FAT PUSS AND FRIENDS

GET SET WITH A READ ALONE!

This entertaining series is designed for all new readers who want to start reading a whole book on their own.

Read Alones may be two or three short stories in one book, or one longer story with chapters, so they are ideal for building reading confidence.

The stories are lively and fun, with lots of illustrations and clear, large type, to make solo reading a perfect pleasure!

By the same author

FAT PUSS AND SLIMPUP
FAT PUSS ON WHEELS

Some other Read Alones for you to enjoy

THE ADVENTURES OF ZOT THE DOG
  Ivan Jones
DODIE   Finola Akister
FINDERS KEEPERS   June Crebbin
GERBIL CRAZY!   Tony Bradman
HELP!   Margaret Gordon
THE KITNAPPING OF MITTENS
  Rebecca Taylor
SAUSAGE MOLE AND LITTLE FOAL
  Diane Redmond
WILLIE WHISKERS   Margaret Gordon

Harriet Castor

Fat Puss
and Friends

Illustrated by Colin West

VIKING

VIKING

Published by the Penguin Group
Penguin Books Ltd, 27 Wrights Lane, London W8 5TZ, England
Penguin Books USA Inc., 375 Hudson Street, New York, New York 10014, USA
Penguin Books Australia Ltd, Ringwood, Victoria, Australia
Penguin Books Canada Ltd, 10 Alcorn Avenue, Toronto, Ontario, Canada M4V 3B2
Penguin Books (NZ) Ltd, 182–190 Wairau Road, Auckland 10, New Zealand

Penguin Books Ltd, Registered Offices: Harmondsworth, Middlesex, England

First published 1984
10 9 8 7 6 5 4

British Library Cataloguing in Publication Data

Castor, Harriet
   Fat Puss and friends.
   I. Title   II. West, Colin
   823'.914[J]   PZ7

ISBN 0–670–81974–3

Typeset in Linotron 202 Century Schoolbook by
Rowland Phototypesetting Ltd, Bury St Edmunds, Suffolk
Made and printed in Great Britain by
Butler & Tanner Ltd, Frome and London

CONTENTS

Fat Puss

Fat Puss was fat. He had little thin
arms, small flat feet, a very short tail
and an amazingly fat tummy.

9

Fat Puss was sad because all his friends teased him about being so fat. He was so enormous that there were lots of things he couldn't do.

Other cats could squeeze through
holes in fencing.

But Fat Puss couldn't.

12

Other cats could jump delicately onto thin bars.

But Fat Puss couldn't.

Other cats could walk through cat flaps.

But Fat Puss couldn't.

Other cats could hide in long grass.

But Fat Puss couldn't.

Other cats could walk about silently.
But Fat Puss couldn't.

One day when Fat Puss was feeling particularly sad, he decided to take a walk to cheer himself up. He plodded along, trying to think of something exciting to do.

Then, just as he came to the top of a hill, Fat Puss tripped over a stone!

And he rolled,

and he rolled,

and he rolled all the way down the hill, right to the bottom.

When Fat Puss finally stopped rolling, he sat up. He had not been hurt at all. In fact he had rather enjoyed his unusual form of travelling.

So when Fat Puss came to the next
hill, he rolled down that too. "Yippee!
This is fun!" he cried.

The next day Fat Puss told all his friends about his great new pastime.

All Fat Puss's friends tried rolling down hills, but because they had such long legs and long tails and were so thin and bony they couldn't roll properly and so got very bruised.

"Oh, we wish we could roll down hills like you, Fat Puss," they said.

Then Fat Puss was happy. He didn't mind that the other cats could do things that he couldn't because at last he had found an exciting thing that he and only he could do!

25

Fat Puss
Finds a Friend

Fat Puss was feeling miserable.
He had been rolling down hills so
much that his tummy was sore. So
he couldn't roll down hills any more
and he had nothing to do.

All Fat Puss's friends were busy
chasing mice.

Fat Puss had tried to chase mice too,
but he could never catch them
because he couldn't run very fast.

Fat Puss felt so miserable that he sat
down in a corner and cried.

Just then Fat Puss heard a little
voice.

"Hello," squeaked the little voice.
Fat Puss looked down. There, in front
of him, sat a small mouse. "Hello,"
said the mouse again.

32

Seeing the mouse made Fat Puss cry
even more. All the other cats could
have caught it but Fat Puss knew
that if he tried to catch the mouse it
would just run away so fast that he
wouldn't even be able to keep up with it.

"What's the matter?" asked the mouse. "I am so slow," sobbed Fat Puss, "that I can't even chase mice like all my friends do."

"I'm very glad about that," said the mouse. This made Fat Puss stop crying for a minute. "Why?" he asked. "Because we mice do not like being chased," replied the mouse.

"Really?" asked Fat Puss, who was very surprised at this.

"Yes," said the mouse, "we'd like cats a lot more if they didn't try to chase us."

"I never knew that," said Fat Puss, cheering up a little. "I suppose it's a good thing that I can't chase mice. Could you be my friend?"

"Of course," said the mouse, "as long as you don't chase me. By the way, my name's Terence."

"My name's Fat Puss," said Fat Puss.

Terence and Fat Puss became very good friends and Fat Puss was very pleased that he had found a companion.

Terence took Fat Puss to meet his wife, Jessica, and his children, Robert and Charlotte.

Fat Puss spent many sunny afternoons playing with the mouse family.

When all the other cats saw what fun
Fat Puss was having they said, "Oh,
we wish we could play with the mice
like you, Fat Puss. But because we
chased them, they won't be friends
with us."

Fat Puss was very, very pleased that he had not done as the other cats had done because now he had made four new friends.

Fat Puss in Summer

One warm summer day the sun was
shining brightly. Fat Puss felt so hot
and thirsty that he sat down for a rest
under a tree.

He saw all the other cats drinking from the pond, stretching their long necks so that they could reach the water without falling in.

Fat Puss wanted a drink very much, so he tried to copy them. He bent down and stretched his neck out as far as he could, but he couldn't reach the water.

He stretched a bit more,

and a bit more,

until all of a sudden,

SPLOSH!!! He tumbled into the pond,
head first.

"What shall I do?" thought Fat Puss.
"I can't swim!"

Soon Fat Puss found that he didn't need to swim.

He was floating.

The other cats saw Fat Puss having
fun floating in the water. So they
tried to float too.

But they were so thin and bony that they couldn't float and they had to scramble quickly to the shore.

They climbed out looking wet and dripping. "We wish we could float in the pond like you, Fat Puss," they said.

Fat Puss was very glad that he could float in the pond. Now he could drink as much as he wanted to and have fun at the same time.

Fat Puss
Meets a Stranger

One day, Fat Puss went for a walk.

He came across a stream which he
had never seen before.

Fat Puss felt very hot, so he decided
to jump in the water and float around
for a while.

He enjoyed himself very much and he
was glad that he had come across this
new stream.

Suddenly, Fat Puss saw a brown,
furry creature swimming towards
him.

It raised its head and he saw that it had very large teeth.

"Oh dear," thought Fat Puss. "What shall I do? There is a brown, furry monster with big, sharp teeth coming towards me and it's going to eat me up!"

Fat Puss could not swim, but he tried to scramble away. The creature was coming nearer and nearer.

Fat Puss closed his eyes and waited for the attack . . .

"Hello," said a friendly voice.

Fat Puss slowly opened his eyes and realized that it was the brown creature who had spoken. "H-hello," returned Fat Puss nervously.

"Don't be afraid," said the creature, "I won't harm you."

"You mean you're not going to eat me up?" asked Fat Puss.

"Why, no, of course not," chuckled the creature. "I don't eat animals, I only eat plants."

Fat Puss felt very relieved.

"My name is Humphrey. I am a beaver," said the creature.

"I am Fat Puss," said Fat Puss.

"Now we know each other better, would you like to come for a swim with me?" asked Humphrey.

"I'm afraid I can't swim," replied Fat Puss sadly. "I can only float."

"I shall teach you how to swim, then!"
exclaimed Humphrey.

"Thank you very much," said Fat
Puss.

Humphrey taught Fat Puss how to swim and they became very good friends.

Fat Puss introduced Humphrey to
Terence Mouse.

Fat Puss was very pleased to have
found a new stream, learned to swim
and to have made another nice new
friend.

Fat Puss at Christmas

One winter morning, Fat Puss went for a walk.

He discovered that everything was covered in something cold and white.

He didn't know what it was, so he went to ask Terence Mouse.

"Oh, that's snow," said Terence. "Don't be afraid of it, it's quite all right." Fat Puss decided to ignore the snow and do what he did every morning: roll down a few hills.

Fat Puss found a hill and began to
roll.

But, as he rolled, the snow stuck to
him and then more snow stuck to this
snow, and soon he looked like a large
snowball.

"Oh dear," thought Fat Puss. "I can't see where I'm going. What shall I do?"

BUMP! It was too late for Fat Puss to do anything.

He had bumped into a little fir tree
and it had knocked all the snow off
him. But the tree had fallen down.

Fat Puss didn't like to leave the tree lying on the hill because somebody else might trip over it. He did not know what to do with it, so he picked it up and took it to show Terence.

"It's a Christmas tree!" said Terence.
"We must decorate it, and then we
can sing carols around it on
Christmas Day."

"Oh, what a lovely idea!" exclaimed
Fat Puss.

Terence collected fir cones and old
leaves and conkers left over from
autumn.

Terence's children, Robert and
Charlotte, painted them bright
colours.

Terence's wife, Jessica, collected milk bottle tops that untidy people had dropped.

Then Fat Puss hung all the things on his tree until it looked gay and pretty.

Then, on Christmas Day, Fat Puss
and the Mouse family all had fun
singing carols around their own
Christmas tree. And Humphrey the
beaver joined them for tea.

The End.